BY THE LIGHT OF THE
HALLOWEEN MOON

CAROLINE STUTSON ~ KEVIN HAWKES

LOTHROP, LEE & SHEPARD BOOKS   NEW YORK

Text copyright © 1993 by
Caroline Stutson. Illustrations
copyright © 1993 by Kevin Hawkes. All
rights reserved. No part of this book may
be reproduced or utilized in any form or by any
means, electronic or mechanical, including photo-
copying and recording, or by any information storage
and retrieval system, without permission in writing from
the Publisher. Inquiries should be addressed to Lothrop, Lee &
Shepard Books, a division of William Morrow & Company, Inc.,
1350 Avenue of the Americas, New York, New York 10019. Printed in the
United States of America. First Edition   3 4 5 6 7 8 9 10

Library of Congress Cataloging in Publication Data. Stutson, Caroline. By the light of the
halloween moon / by Caroline Stutson ; illustrated by Kevin Hawkes. p. cm.   Summary:
In this cumulative story, a cat's pursuit of a toe sets off a chain of events. ISBN 0-688-12045-8.
—ISBN 0-688-12046-6 (lib. bdg.) [1. Halloween—Fiction.] I. Hawkes, Kevin, ill. II. Title.
PZ7.S9416By 1993 [E]—dc20 92-10258 CIP AC

For A.C., Chris, Al, and Randy—C.S.
For Susan Pearson—K.H.

A toe!
A lean and gleaming toe
That taps a tune in the dead of night
By the light, by the light,
By the silvery light of the Halloween moon!

A cat!
A thin black wisp of a spying cat
Who eyes the toe
That taps a tune in the dead of night
By the light, by the light,
By the silvery light of the Halloween moon!

A witch!
A watchful witch with streaming hair
Who snatches the cat
When he springs through the air to catch the toe
That taps a tune in the dead of night
By the light, by the light,
By the silvery light of the Halloween moon!

A bat!
A bungling bouncy breezy bat

Who bumps the witch as she snatches the cat
When he springs through the air to catch the toe
That taps a tune in the dead of night
By the light, by the light,
By the silvery light of the Halloween moon!

Who swats at the bat
Who bumps the witch as she snatches the cat
When he springs through the air to catch the toe
That taps a tune in the dead of night
By the light, by the light,
By the silvery light of the Halloween moon!

A ghost!
A williwaw ghost

Who trips the ghoul
Who swats at the bat
Who bumps the witch as she snatches the cat
When he springs through the air to catch the toe
That taps a tune in the dead of night
By the light, by the light,
By the silvery light of the Halloween moon!

A sprite!
A grumpy grungy hobgoblin sprite

Who bites the ghost
Who trips the ghoul
Who swats at the bat
Who bumps the witch as she snatches the cat
When he springs through the air to catch the toe
That taps a tune in the dead of night
By the light, by the light,
By the silvery light of the Halloween moon!

A girl!
A small bright slip of a smiling girl

Who smacks the sprite
Who bites the ghost
Who trips the ghoul
Who swats at the bat
Who bumps the witch as she snatches the cat
When he springs through the air to catch the toe
That taps a tune in the dead of night

OH, NO YOU DON'T!
THAT TOE IS MINE!

By the light, by the light,
By the silvery light of the Halloween moon!